How Frank Helped Hank

Written by Suzanne Hemming
Illustrated by Jacquie Hughes
Book design by Oliver McQuitty

First published in 2020 by Thea Chops Books
www.theachopsbooks.com

A catalogue record for this book is available from the British Library
ISBN 978-0-9957259-3-5

Printed in Great Britain by Doveton Press Ltd on FSC certified paper
TCB013

How Frank Helped Hank

For Thea

On a hot afternoon, in the middle of June,
a family went out for the day.
A dad called Hank, his son named Frank,
and Frank's little sister called May.

They walked through a park;
where kids played and dogs barked,
excited about their day out.
Passing benches and trees, and a hive full of bees,
when they suddenly heard someone shout:

"Look out!
Watch the ball!" a young girl had called.

As Frank glanced up and then froze.
He widened his eyes,
and then quite the surprise,
the ball hit him hard on the nose!

Making no sound, Frank dropped to the ground,
then let out a really big sigh:

"My nose really hurts,

this pain is the worst"

and poor Frank started to cry.

Frank's dad shouted,

"Oy! None of that boy!"

He had such a scowl on his face!
"Man up son! Rule number one!
Never cry in a public place!"

Frank felt so sad, 'cause here was his dad,
who was always saying, "man up".
Pushing tears to one side, and swallowing pride,
Frank gave his sore nose a good rub.

Onwards they walked, and though no-one talked,
everyone felt a bit sad.
Frank a bit glum, and May keeping shtum,
even Hank also felt pretty bad.

See when Hank was small, he fell off a wall,
and he broke his leg and his wrist!
Though he wanted to cry, he had wiped his eyes dry,
as his mum had shouted, "Desist!

Man up!" She had said, shaking her head,
"Don't let your dad see your tears.
Only girls cry out loud, and boys should be proud,
to never show weakness or fears!"

So now Hank was grown with a son of his own,
and they walked on their family day out.

Through the park,
past the trees,
and the hive full of bees,
to visit the butterfly house.

What beautiful things these butterfly wings,
as they flittered and fluttered around.
They glistened and gleamed, in the sparkly sunbeams,
and everyone watched them spellbound.

After a while, all beaming with smiles,
as the butterflies fluttered non stop.
Hank nodded his head, "Time's up" he said,
and they exited through the gift shop.

13

The shop although small, was filled wall to wall,
with plenty of butterfly things.
A wing-shaped mat and a colourful hat,
and dress-up butterfly wings!

May picked the wings and a butterfly ring,
but something else caught Frank's eye:

a wand that shimmered, it glistened and glimmered;
he knew what he wanted to buy!

"Look dad!", called out Frank, waving at Hank,
"This wand looks like butterfly wings!"
"Put it down!" shouted Hank, looking sternly at Frank,
"Only little girls play with such things!"

Frank felt so sad, because of his dad,
who was always complaining, he'd say:
"Boys shouldn't cry; they should all be tough guys,
only little girls act in that way!"

See Frank had once thought,
these things he'd be been taught,
about boys and girls by his dad.

But his friend named Flo,
who was more in the know,
had explained to him
that was all mad.

"Boys shouldn't cry?!
Says who?!" Flo would sigh.
That doesn't sound healthy to me!
Let the tears flow; let all feelings show;
now that is the best way to be!

So May and Frank, and their dad called Hank
headed back through the park walking home.
Passing benches and trees and the hive full of bees,
and a dog who was chewing a bone.

"Watch out! Watch the ball!" they heard someone call.

They all turned their heads to the shout.
The ball missed Frank but squarely hit Hank,
and he fell to the floor and passed out!

He quickly came round and made whimpering sounds,
holding his head with his hand.
"I'm fine", he cried as he swallowed his pride,
and unsteadily started to stand.

Hank wouldn't admit, as he wobbled a bit,
that his head was really quite sore.
Stumbling back he heard something crack:
and they all looked down on the floor.

Hank made a groan, he had stepped on the bone,
of a nearby dog who looked glum.
First the dog howled, and then the dog growled,
and he gave Hank a bite on the bum!

"I'm fine!" Hank lied, feeling quite mortified!
He took a step back and then froze,
he had knocked his knee on the hive full of bees,

and a bee stung him right on the nose!

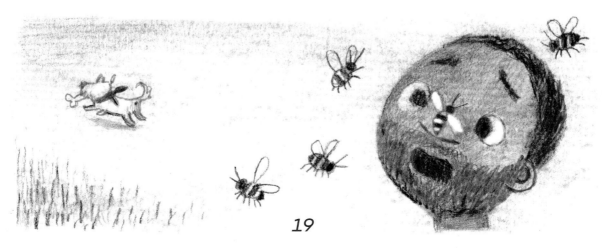

"It's fine!" said Hank while looking at Frank,
 so determined that he wouldn't cry.
"But Daddy," said Frank, softly to Hank,
"Daddy I think that's a lie.

Your head got hit, and your bottom got bit,
and your nose got stung by a bee.
Let it out, have a cry, don't keep it inside,
it will help you feel better, you'll see."

See Frank's friend Flo,
well she's in the know,
about loving who you are inside;
"For good mental health,
you should just be yourself."

Hank smiled at his son and replied,

"So, to cry is ok? And you like wands eh?
Your friend Flo: she seems bright!
What my parents thought, it's just what they were taught,
'Cause you wouldn't hold laughter in, right?!"

And so a boy named Frank,
helped a dad called Hank,
by saying it's ok to cry.
That being yourself,
is good for your health,
Why don't you give it a try?

The End